THIS BLOOMSBURY BOOK

BELONGS TO

....

To Emma – SG

For the little white duck that lives in Windsor – NL

This edition published for Igloo Books Ltd in 2007

First published in Great Britain in 2002 by Bloomsbury Publishing Plc
38 Soho Square, London, W1D 3HB

A CIP catalogue record of this book is available from the British Library
ISBN 0 7475 6110 9

Designed by Sarah Hodder

Printed in China

10 9 8 7 6 5 4 3 2

Mucky Duck

Sally Grindley
Illustrations by Neal Layton

Oliver Dunkley had a pond in his garden, and on that pond lived Mucky Duck.

Mucky Duck was supposed to be white,
and sometimes she was, but mostly she wasn't.
And this is why...

Mucky Duck liked cooking. Pouring and mixing, rolling and shaping.

O you Mucky Duck!

Mucky Duck liked football. Dribbling and tackling, shooting and diving.

Mucky Duck liked painting. Dipping
and sponging, squirting and splattering.

O you Mucky Duck!

Mucky Duck liked gardening. Digging and weeding, planting and sowing.

O you Mucky Duck!

So once every week Mucky Duck had to have a bath.
Wash, wipe, rub, scrub.
And Mucky Duck didn't like that.

Who's a clean Mucky Duck then!

But not for long!

Acclaim for *Mucky Duck*

'Any three-year-old who loves painting, grubbing about in the garden, cooking and generally getting dirty all over, will identify with this charmingly mucky duck and the cheerfully chaotic, but wonderful illustrations' *Daily Mail*

Enjoy more great picture books from Sally Grindley and Neal Layton …

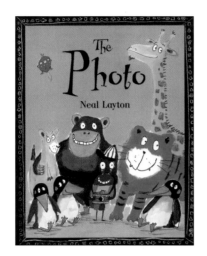

The Photo
Neal Layton

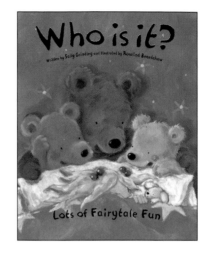

Who is It?
Sally Grindley & Rosalind Beardshaw

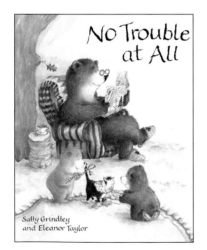

No Trouble at All
Sally Grindley & Eleanor Taylor

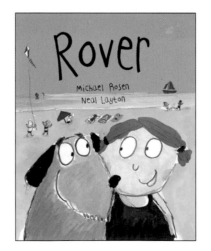

Rover
Michael Rosen & Neal Layton

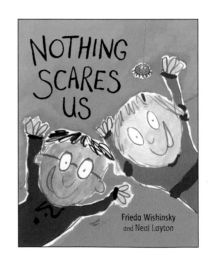

Nothing Scares Us
Frieda Wishinsky & Neal Layton

All titles are available in paperback priced £4.99